PZ
7
.C88722
W5
2005

P9-CCY-536

For Holly
—D. C.

For Karina Anastasia
—S. M.

Atheneum Books for Young Readers
An imprint of Simon & Schuster Children's Publishing Division
1230 Avenue of the Americas
New York, New York 10020
Text copyright © 2005 by Doreen Cronin
Illustrations copyright © 2005 by Scott Menchin
All rights reserved, including the right of reproduction
in whole or in part in any form.
Book design by Polly Kanevsky and Kristin Smith
The text of this book is set in Bliss.
The illustrations for this book are rendered digitally.
Manufactured in China
First Edition
10 9 8 7 6 5 4 3 2 1
Library of Congress Cataloging-in-Publication Data
Cronin, Doreen.
Wiggle / Doreen Cronin ; illustrated by Scott Menchin.— 1st ed.
p. cm.
Summary: Rhyming text describes the many ways to wiggle.
ISBN 0-689-86375-6
[1. Dance—Fiction. 2. Stories in rhyme.] I. Menchin, Scott, ill. II. Title.
PZ8.3.C879   Wi 2005
[E]—dc22 2004003326

170301

Wiggle

doreen cronin
ART BY
SCOTT MENCHIN

Atheneum Books for Young Readers
New York London Toronto Sydney

RECEIV

MAY — 2006

SENECA LIBRARIES
KING CAMPUS

RECEIVED MAY 12

Do you wake up wake up

with a wiggle?

it might **wind up** on your head.

First wiggle where your

tail would be.

Feeling **extra** silly?

Can you
wiggle

with
your
shadow?

Can you **wiggle** with your toys?

When you
wiggle

with gorillas,

do they

make

a wiggle

noise?

Can you **wiggle** in the water?

open
big
and
wide.

When
you
wiggle
where
your
wings
would be,

wiggles
fill the sky.

Wiggle **slowly** when with polar bears.

They're very wiggle shy.

Snakes are one **big** wiggle.

No wings.

No tails.

No feet.

Some wiggles are worth waiting for . . .

Would you join me for a wiggle?

Would you **wiggle** on the **moon?**

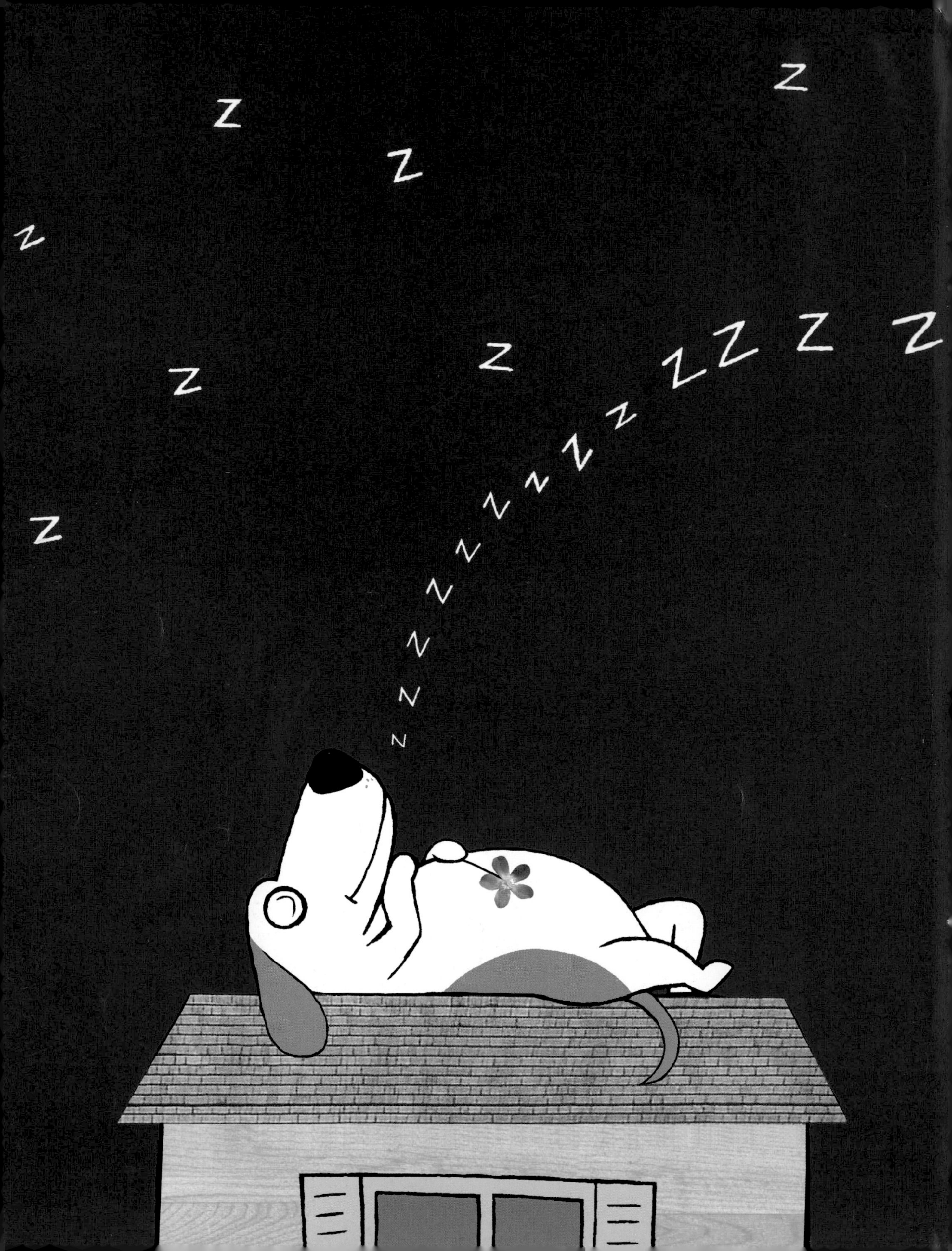

I think
we're out
of wiggles
now.

See you
wiggle
soon!

PROPERTY OF
SENECA COLLEGE
LIBRARIES
KING CAMPUS